Old Mother Hubbard

For Paula

Based on The Comic Adventures of *Old Mother Hubbard and Her Dog*, by Sarah Catherine Martin, originally published in London, 1805, by John Harris.

ISBN 0-439-46512-5

12 11 10 9 8 7 6 5 4 3 2 1   2 3 4 5 6 7/0

Printed in the U.S.A.   14

First Scholastic printing, November 2002

Jane Cabrera

Old
Mother
Hubbard

SCHOLASTIC INC.

New York   Toronto   London   Auckland   Sydney
Mexico City   New Delhi   Hong Kong   Buenos Aires

to fetch
her poor
dog

a bone.

But when she got there, the cupboard was bare, and so the poor dog had none.

She went to
the tailor's

to buy him
a coat.

But when she came back, he was riding a goat.

She went to
the hatter's

to buy him
a hat.

But when she came back, he was washing the cat.

But when she came back, he was dancing a jig.

She went to
the cobbler's

to buy him
some shoes.

But when
she came back,
he was reading
the news.

Then the
dame made
a curtsy,

The dog made a bow.